HIKE
WANDER
PACE
PLOD
ROAM
PACE
STRANDER
WANDER
SHUFFLE
MEANDER
STROLL
TRAIPSE
RAMBLE
MARCH
HIKE
STROLL
AMBLE
TRAIPSE
RAMBLE
MARCH
PACE
WANDER
STRANDER
MEANDER
PLOD
ROAM

KU-493-254

When you TAKE A Step

Bethanie Deeney Murguia

Beach Lane Books · New York   London   Toronto   Sydney   New Delhi

BEACH LANE BOOKS
An imprint of Simon & Schuster Children's Publishing Division
1230 Avenue of the Americas, New York, New York 10020
© 2022 by Bethanie Deeney Murguia
Jacket design by Sonia Chaghatzbanian and Rebecca Syracuse © 2022 by Simon & Schuster, Inc.
All rights reserved, including the right of reproduction in whole or in part in any form.
BEACH LANE BOOKS and colophon are trademarks of Simon & Schuster, Inc.
For information about special discounts for bulk purchases, please contact
Simon & Schuster Special Sales at 1-866-506-1949 or business@simonandschuster.com.
The Simon & Schuster Speakers Bureau can bring authors to your live event. For more information or to book an event,
contact the Simon & Schuster Speakers Bureau at 1-866-248-3049 or visit our website at www.simonspeakers.com.
Interior design by Rebecca Syracuse
The text for this book was set in Caslon Manuscript.
The illustrations for this book were rendered digitally.
Manufactured in China
0522 SCP
First Edition
2 4 6 8 10 9 7 5 3 1
Library of Congress Cataloging-in-Publication Data
Names: Murguia, Bethanie Deeney, author, illustrator.
Title: When you take a step / Bethanie Deeney Murguia.
Description: First edition. | New York : Beach Lane Books, [2022] | Audience: Ages 0-8 | Audience: Grades 2-3 | Summary:
"To take a walk is to begin a journey. It can be an adventure, or a chance to let your thoughts roam and be one with nature.
It can be a time for daydreaming and pondering life's many questions. It can be a time to reflect on the past or to stand
up for a better future."— Provided by publisher.
Identifiers: LCCN 2021022423 (print) | LCCN 2021022424 (ebook) | ISBN 9781534473676 (hardcover) |
ISBN 9781534473683 (ebook)
Subjects: CYAC: Self-actualization (Psychology)—Fiction. | Self-confidence—Fiction.
Classification: LCC PZ7.M944 Wh 2022 (print) | LCC PZ7.M944 (ebook) | DDC [E]—dc23
LC record available at https://lccn.loc.gov/2021022423
LC ebook record available at https://lccn.loc.gov/2021022424

For my hiking friends—thank you
for sharing the path

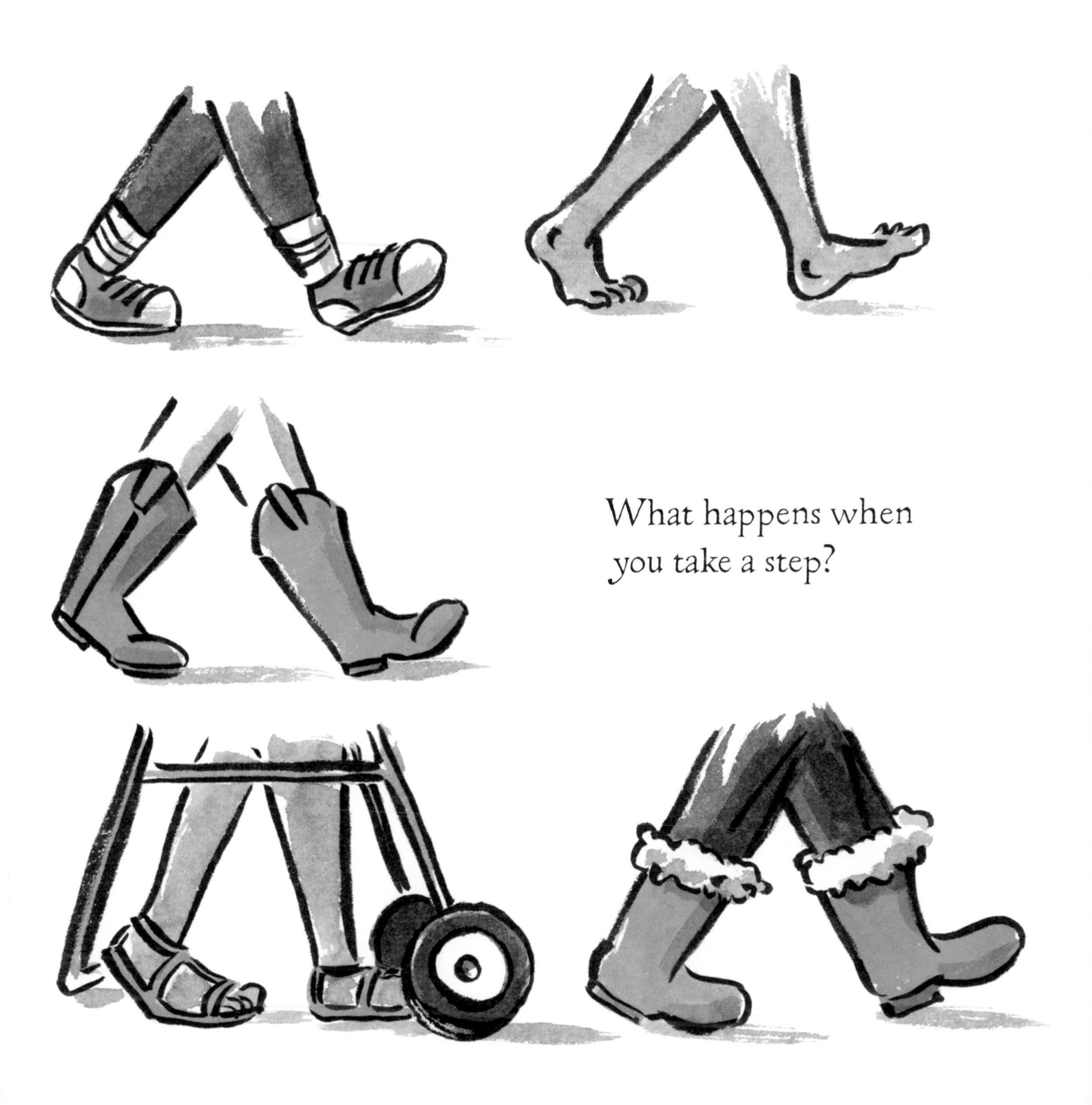

What happens when
you take a step?

You begin a journey.

You find your balance.

You greet the world, wide and full.

You crunch fall leaves.

You collect small treasures.

You make new friends,
wild and free.

You share a path.

You join the rhythm.

You gather courage and try again.

You follow your heart.

You blaze a trail.

You begin to dream, big and bold.

You learn from your heroes.

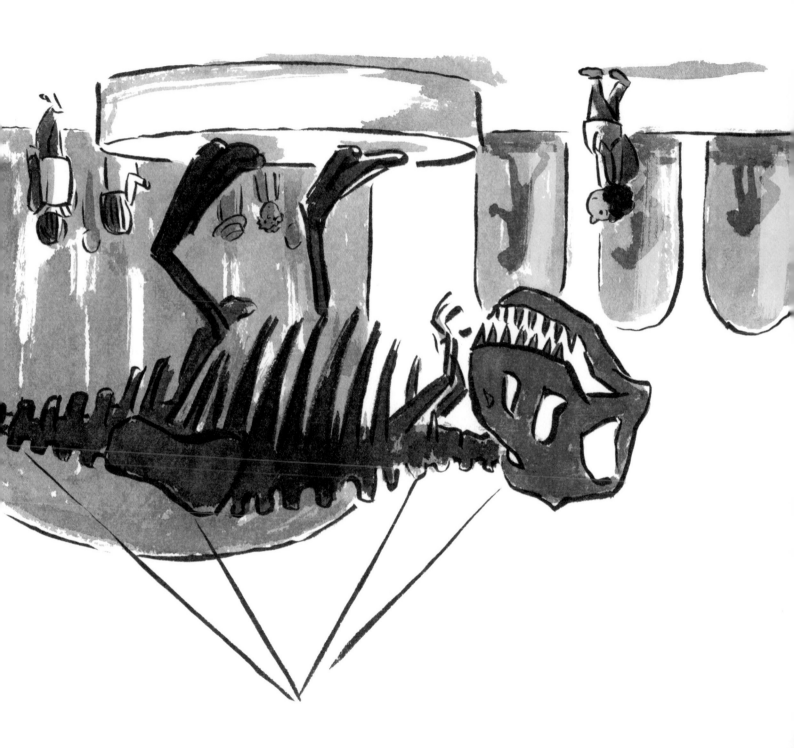

You meet the past.

You walk with all who have
walked before.

You discover your power.

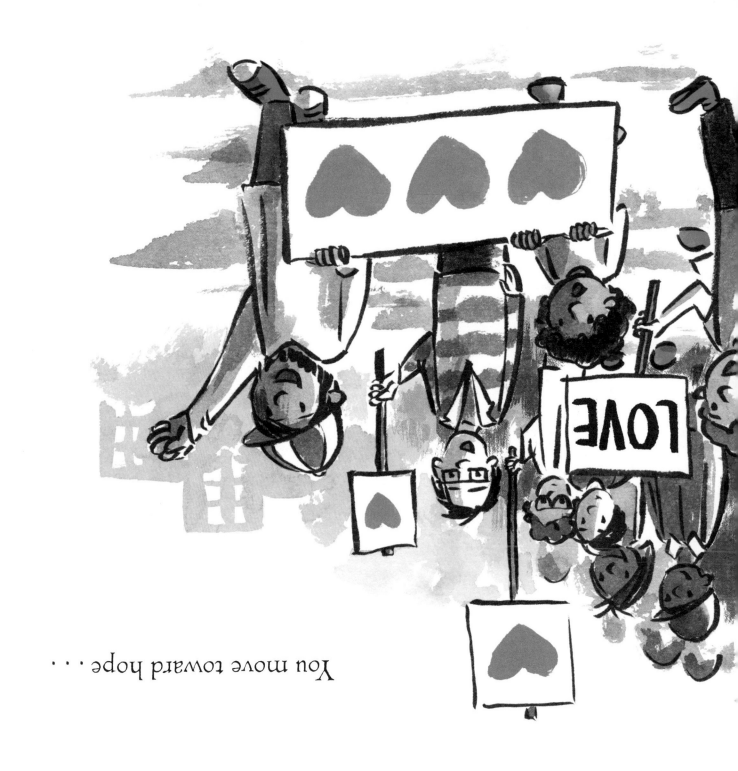

You move toward hope . . .

and you make the world better . . .

when you take a step.

MARCH

ROAM

RAMBLE

PLOD

TRAIPSE

HIKE

stroll

meander

SHUFFLE

SLOG

meander

Wander

PACE

MARCH

ROAM

RAMBLE

TRUDGE

PLOD

TRAIPSE

HIKE

stroll

SLOG

Wander

PACE